Caution: Turtles and Frogs Ahead!

by Joanne Mattern with Maxime Bonneau

RED CHAIR PRESS
Egremont, Massachusetts

RED CHAIR PRESS
BOOKS FOR YOUNG READERS

Wildlife Rescue is produced and published by Red Chair Press:
Red Chair Press LLC PO Box 333 South Egremont, MA 01258-0333
www.redchairpress.com

Publisher's Cataloging-In-Publication Data
Names: Mattern, Joanne, 1963- author.
Title: Caution : turtles and frogs ahead! / by Joanne Mattern.

Description: South Egremont, MA : Red Chair Press, [2022] | Series: Wildlife rescue | Interest age level: 007-010. | Includes index and suggested resources for further reading. | Summary: "Reptiles and amphibians need special help crossing roads. This book focuses on different approaches, from tiny turtle tunnels under railroad tracks in Japan, to salamander tunnels and turtle crossing guards in the U.S., to toad tunnels in the UK, and bucket brigades for frogs and toads in France"--Provided by publisher.

Identifiers: ISBN 9781643711898 (hardcover) | ISBN 9781643711935 (softcover) | ISBN 9781643711973 (ePDF) | ISBN 9781643712017 (ePub 3 S&L) | ISBN 9781643712055 (ePub 3 TR) | ISBN 9781643712093 (Kindle)

Subjects: LCSH: LCSH: Wildlife crossings--Juvenile literature. | Wildlife habitat improvement--Juvenile literature. | Reptiles--Conservation--Juvenile literature. | Amphibians--Conservation--Juvenile literature. | Animals and civilization--Juvenile literature. | CYAC: Wildlife habitat improvement. | Reptiles. | Amphibians. | Animals and civilization.

Classification: LCC SK356.W54 M382 2022 (print) | LCC SK356.W54 (ebook) | DDC 333.95/416--dc23

LC record available at: https://lccn.loc.gov/2021945551

Photo credits: Cover, p. 6, 8–11, 13, 20, 24, 25, 27: iStock; p. 1, 4, 5, 7, 8, 16, 17, 28: Shutterstock; p. 20–23, 26 (inset): Maxime Bonneau; p. 12, 14, 18, 19: Jane Aguilar Murphy; p. 15, 26: Carolyn Hill

Printed in United States of America
0422 1P CGF22

Table of Contents

Snapping Turtles and Friends

Common snapping turtles live all over the eastern part of the United States and southeastern Canada. These turtles got their name because they have big, sharp jaws. Snapping turtles like to swim. They always live near and in water.

Danger for Turtles

Turtles often cross roads while trying to find a dry place to lay their eggs. When the young turtles hatch, they go back across the road to find a wet place to live. Turtles are often hit by cars as they walk across the road.

After digging a hole in dry soil, the female lays 25 to 80 eggs each year. She guides them into the nest with her back feet and covers them with dirt.

A newly hatched turtle has dug its way to the surface and will look for water.

Crossing a road is very dangerous for slow-moving turtles.

In 2007, Carolyn Hill and her family moved to Western Highway in Blauvelt, New York. They were excited to see snapping turtles. But their happiness did not last. Carolyn saw many turtles getting hit by cars on the busy road. She decided to help the turtles.

Why Did the Turtle Cross the Road?

Carolyn found out that the turtles lived in a **reservoir** on one side of the road. The ground there was too wet to lay their eggs. So, they crossed Western Highway and laid eggs on the other side.

While they live in many parts of North America, the common snapping turtle is New York State's official reptile.

They may be slow, but snapping turtles can bite off a finger!

Crossing Guards

Carolyn and her family made signs. Her family and friends stopped traffic when they saw turtles crossing. They stood in the road so the turtles could cross safely. More friends helped. They called their group The Turtles of Western Highway.

FAST FACTS:

Snapping turtles are active hunters that prey on anything they can swallow, including fish, frogs, reptiles (such as snakes and smaller turtles), birds, and small mammals.

They also help keep the water clean by eating overgrown plants and **decayed** fish.

XING
SLOW

The local library told people about Carolyn's group. The local government told the community too. The county highway department put up cones and signs so drivers would slow down.

Tiny Hatchlings

Carolyn also wanted to help the baby turtles, or **hatchlings**. After hatching from their eggs, the babies crossed the road to get to the water. The tiny turtles looked like leaves on the road. Cars often hit them. So, Carolyn and her friends carried the hatchlings across. Girl Scouts and school children came to help.

New Homes

Carolyn got a big idea from a turtle doctor who knew a lot about keeping turtles safe. She and her group built nesting mounds near the reservoir. They also built a fence so the turtles could not cross the road. The turtles liked the nesting mounds. Most of them laid their eggs there. Now there were not so many turtles crossing the road!

The turtles liked their new nesting mounds.

Frog Crossing

People in Beuvardes, France, are helping animals too. In 2008, they put up a fence along the road. They put buried buckets along the fence. During the night, frogs and salamanders try to cross the road to get to a pond. They fall into the buckets instead.

Buried buckets help keep frogs and salamanders off the road.

The Beuvardes Bucket Buddies at work!

The next morning, people check the buckets. They count the **amphibians** inside. Then they carry the animals safely across the road and release them, or let them go into the pond.

Terrific Tunnels!

Many places have built tunnels to help frogs, toads, and turtles. In Japan, tiny tunnels run under train tracks. In Amherst, Massachusetts, there are tunnels to help salamanders cross a busy road to a pond. England, Wales, and California all have toad tunnels to save frogs and toads from crossing busy roads.

Plastic fencing helps direct frogs to use the tunnel under this road.

This tunnel in Hallau, Switzerland, was built just for frogs to get to a wetland on the other side of the road.

Saving Lives

People like Carolyn Hill and Clémance Lambert and others around the world are saving lives. They work together to protect turtles, frogs, toads, and salamanders. Their work makes the world a better—and safer!—place.

Clémance Lambert manages the Beuvardes bucket rescue.

Glossary

amphibians: creatures like frogs, toads, and salamanders who live part of their lives in water and part of their lives on land

decayed: old or rotten, broken down

hatchlings: baby turtles

reservoir: a large lake used as a public water supply

Learn More in the Library

Carstairs, Sue. *Saving Turtles: A Kids' Guide to Endangered Creatures*. Firefly Books, 2014.

Hughes, Catherine. *Little Kids First Book of Reptiles and Amphibians*. National Geographic, 2020.

Messner, Kate. *Tracking Tortoises, The Mission to Save a Galapagos Giant*, Millbrook Press, 2022.

Wilsdon, Christina. *Ultimate Reptileopedia*. National Geographic, 2015.

Index

About the Author

Joanne Mattern is the author of many books for children including the Core Content: ***Earth's Amazing Animals Series***. She loves writing about sports, all kinds of animals, and interesting people. Mattern lives in New York State with her family.